come play with me

BY

MABEL WATTS

Korsch Munich

Korsch Munich

Oh, oh, everything's going!
Balls are bouncing,
pups are pouncing,
leaves are wiggling,
grass is jiggling,
tails are waggling,
worms are wriggling,
flowers are swaying,
children are playing,
clothes are blowing—
EVERYTHING'S going!

(Going, going! What shall I chase?)

Little dogs have little barks.

They do not scare away burglars.

They do not pull children's wagons.

They do not herd sheep or stand guard with policemen.

Little dogs are lap-size.

They are soft and warm.

They will wear ribbons—sometimes—for a minute or two.

Korsch Munich

Tell me a story.
Tell me a story about a kitten
who lived in a palace
and slept on a silken cushion.
Was she a brown and white kitten?
With big blue eyes?
I like that story.

Look at us. Look at how quiet we are.
We would rather be scratching up pansies,
or chewing up shoe laces,
or batting the telephone off the hook.
Look!
We are being good as gold, so no one will scold,
but who wants to sit? Is it fun?
NOT A BIT!

Let's play IF.

If it is a mouse I'll chase it.

If it is a doll I'll jump on it.

If it is a ball I'll pat it.

If it is a dog—

If it is a DOG,

I'll run under the bed and hide

while you make the dog go away.

Korsch Munich

Korsch Munich

I hear someone in our doghouse. Do you?

Yes, I do!

Is it a squirrel looking for his lunch?

Is it a hen laying an egg?

Is there a mouse in our house?

The cat is there! You chase her out.

No, you do it.

SCAT, CAT!

No place to curl up.
No place to play.
No cat fish, no milk dish . . . .
We're moving today.
Don't forget my ball, Mr. Moving Man.
Don't forget my blanket or my red catnip mouse.
Don't forget to take them to the other house.

Korsch Munich

My furry coat feels just right on a snowy day
or a frosty night.
But when the sun is hot
I'd like to splash with you in a cool, cool pool.
I'd like you to pet me
and brush me
while we sit in the shade.
I'd like that a lot.

What kind of cat would I like to be?
A candy-shop cat? A Halloween cat?
A grocery-store cat? A prize cat? A wise cat?
Know what kind of cat I'd like to be?
Why, a sailor cat who goes out to sea!
(I'd sail to a country far away
and I'd order sardines for my breakfast tray!)

Korsch Munich

My! What tall, straight ears we have
(to hear you calling us for lunch).
Oh! What big green eyes we have
(to see you pouring our cream).
Look! What handy long tails we have
(just right to wrap around our paws
and noses when we curl up to go to sleep).

Korsch Munich

Listen! I hear children playing in the park!
Will someone please brush the hair from my eyes
so I can *see* them?
There, that's better. Now open the gate
and I'll bark at the children so they'll wait.

Wuff, wuff, I'm coming!

When I'm sitting like this,
with nothing much to do,
I pretend I'm a tiger
living at the zoo—
a wild tiger, in a cage,
looking out at YOU.

Do you think I look like a tiger?

Who is that in the mirror?

Is it Mother Hubbard's dog?

Is it little Tommy Tucker's dog?

Maybe it isn't a dog at all.

Maybe it's a . . . .

What can it be?

Oh, I see—ME!

Oops! Look what I've done!
Now someone is coming.
Someone with clumpy footsteps,
and someone with clicky footsteps,
and someone with skippy steps, too.
Clump, clump,
    click, click,
        skippety skip.

(They'll see what I did. Guess it's time that I hid.)

I'm too big to sit in the laundry basket,
too big to sit on the chairs,
too big to stretch out on beds, or on stairs.
I'm not even able to squeeze under the table.
But look! I am FRIEND-size.
Just try me!

Ho-hum, we're sitting in our basket,
all ready for bed.
We've had such a busy day.
We played with spools strung on a cord.
We hid behind doors
and jumped out at people.
We tangled up Grandma's wool.
    And now we want to sleep,
    and dream about mint beds
    and milk pans. And mice.
Ho-hum, we're sitting in our basket,
all ready for bed . . . .

Won't you please come and tuck us in?

We're not very tall.
We're not a bit curly.
We're the kind of dogs who wake up early
to pull off your blankets
and tickle your toe.
That's our way of saying "Good morning"
and "Hello."

Come on, Lazy Bones, get up!

I'd like to look for things for you—
your kite, your cap, your long-lost shoe.
Throw a ball and I'll bring it back
(bragging, tail a-wagging).
I'll bring you sticks and stones, too.
(But the bones I'd rather keep
to hide under my pillow when I sleep.)

Where's Mother?

There's Mother Cat washing her kittens.

There's Mother Duck teaching her ducklings to swim.

There's Mother Horse playing with her colt.

And we are waiting for *our* mother. Waiting and waiting.

Here she comes!

We can hardly believe it but it's true.

It's true!

We hid behind a door and pounced out at a mouse.

Then the mouse hid behind a door and pounced out
at us!

He flipped his tail, skipped into his hole,
and that was that.

(You'd look surprised, too, if you were a cat!)

Korsch Munich

Do you know what?
I can shake hands—shut a door—ROLL OVER!
Do you know what?
I can sit up on my hind legs
and balance a cooky on my nose.
Do you know what? I'd like to show you.
I'd like to *know* you.